Animal Crackers

A Tender Book About
Death and Funerals and Love

By: Bridget Marshall
Designed by: Ron Boldt,
New Idea Design

ISBN#1-56123-101-0
SAN#298-1815

A Centering Corporation Resource
1531 N. Saddle Creek Rd.
Omaha, NE 68104
Phone: 402-553-1200
Fax: 402-553-0507
E-mail: J1200@aol.com

Animal Crackers

Nanny lives in a big house,
It's not too far away.
And when we go to visit her,
She has a fun game we play.

She hides things in the sofa,
Or tucked inside our beds.
And we find toys where we sit down,
Or in the pillows under our heads.

Sometimes we find candy,
Sometimes we find treats,
Sometimes we find animal crackers,
Hidden under seats.

Nanny smiles when she sees us,
And laughs as we search all around
For M&M's and bubble gum
That we know must be found.

Sometimes she plays piano,
And sometimes she will sing.
Going to my Nanny's house
Is my very favorite thing!

Our Nanny hugged us a lot.
She laughed a lot.
She loved us
and she loved animal crackers.

Nanny had a secret candy bowl in her parlor.
It was hidden behind her curtains.
It was always full of M&M's when we got there.
While Nanny talked to Mom and Dad,
my brother and I filled our mouths
and our pockets
with M&M's.

1

Nanny liked to hide things.
After we found the candy dish, we had to find
the animal crackers.
Sometimes she hid them behind her sofa.
Sometimes she hid them in her cabinet.
They could be anywhere in her wonderful, big old house.
We loved Nanny's hiding places.
We loved Nanny, too.

In school our teacher told us to write a poem.
It had to be about our favorite person, place or thing.
It was easy for me.
I wrote a poem about Nanny
and her big old house
and her hiding places
and her animal crackers.

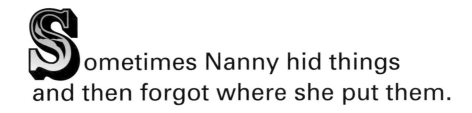ometimes Nanny hid things
and then forgot where she put them.

We thought it was funny and made it part of the game.

One day Nanny hid her false teeth.
We found them in the sofa.

But then Nanny forgot to turn the stove off
and burned up her best pan.
She forgot she'd taken her medicine
and took it twice.

Mom and Dad were worried.
After Nanny fell and hurt herself,
they said it wasn't safe for her to live
all alone in her big house.

3

Nanny went to live in a nursing home.
People there were very nice.
They took care of Nanny so she wouldn't fall and get hurt
and so she wouldn't forget important things.

Nanny liked the people
but she missed her house with the big front porch.
She missed her flowers and her piano.
She said her roomate snored.
Nanny snored, too.

Her candy dish didn't have candy in it anymore.
Nanny kept her medicine in it.

But she still kept animal crackers in her room.
We found them in her dresser.
We found them beside her bed.

4

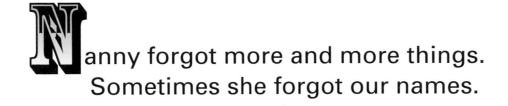anny forgot more and more things.
Sometimes she forgot our names.

We showed her pictures of us when we were younger.
She said we looked a lot like the children in the pictures.

One day we saw our mom hiding
animal crackers in Nanny's dresser.
We knew she couldn't even remember
her animal crackers now.

Nanny didn't get out of bed.
She didn't talk much.
Mom and Dad said she was very old and very tired.
They said our Nanny would die soon.

One day I went to the store after school.
I took my whole allowance.
I bought animal crackers for Nanny.
Animal crackers always made me feel good.
I thought they would make Nanny feel better, too.
I took them home and told Mom and Dad
I wanted to take them to Nanny.

Mom started to cry.
She said they were waiting for me to come home.
The nursing home had called while I was gone.
Nanny had died that afternoon.

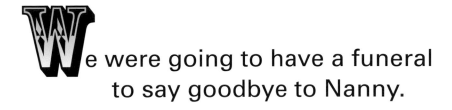

We were going to have a funeral
to say goodbye to Nanny.

I didn't want to say good-bye.
I wanted to share my animal crackers with her.
I wanted Nanny to be back in her big house.
I wanted to find her M&M's again.

But that wasn't going to happen,
and that made me angry and sad.

I went to the funeral with my mom and dad and brother.
In my purple purse, I had my poem I had written in school.
I had the box of animal crackers I had bought.

I wasn't hungry, but looking at the animal crackers
made me think of Nanny.

7

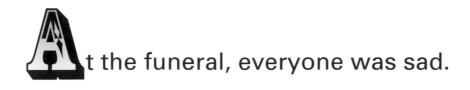

At the funeral, everyone was sad.

Some people talked about Nanny.
Some people cried.
Everyone missed her.

My dad said he was going to say something about Nanny.
He asked me if I wanted to say anything.
I handed him my poem.
He smiled at me.
He went up in front of all the people.
He said I had written about Nanny in school.
He read my poem to everyone there.

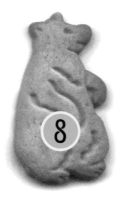

8

My dad remembered the animal crackers, too.
He bent down and picked up a big bag.
It was full of boxes of animal crackers.
Dad asked my brother and me
to pass them out to everyone
who had come to say good-bye to Nanny.

Nanny's friend Marge, sniffled and put the box in her purse.
My baby cousin Sara, took her box and screeched,
"Nanny Crackers! Nanny Crackers!"
Everyone could hear her.

My brother laughed and tore his box open
and started to eat them.
Everyone was laughing and
remembering Nanny.

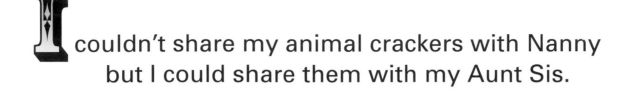couldn't share my animal crackers with Nanny
but I could share them with my Aunt Sis.

She laughed and said they reminded her of Nanny.
She said Nanny used to hide animal crackers
for her and my dad to find.
She was glad we all had animal crackers
to share together
one more time.

I still miss Nanny.
Animal crackers always remind me of her.
I remember her smile and her hugs.
I remember the candy dish full of M&M's
just like my heart is full of memories of her.